SpongeBob MoviePants

by James Gelsey

Illustrated by Gregg Schigiel

SCHOLASTIC INC.

New York   Toronto   London   Auckland   Sydney
Mexico City   New Delhi   Hong Kong   Buenos Aires

No part of this publication may be reproduced in whole or in part,
or stored in a retrieval system, or transmitted in any form or by
any means, electronic, mechanical, photocopying, recording,
or otherwise, without written permission of the publisher.

Published by Scholastic Inc.,
90 Old Sherman Turnpike, Danbury, Connecticut 06816.

SCHOLASTIC and associated logos are trademarks
and/or registered trademarks of Scholastic Inc.

ISBN 0-439-56268-6

First Scholastic Printing, September 2003

Chapters

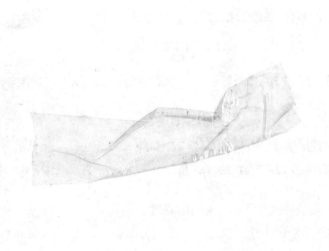

One day, SpongeBob SquarePants and his best friend, Patrick Star, were walking home from the movies.

"That was the best movie ever," SpongeBob said. "I laughed. I cried."

"I cried, too," Patrick admitted.

"Only after you spilled your popcorn," SpongeBob pointed out.

"That was so sad," Patrick sobbed, blowing his nose.

SpongeBob wondered how he could make people laugh and cry.

Patrick thought for a moment. "You could tickle folks and then rub them with sandpaper," he suggested helpfully.

"Or I can make a movie!" SpongeBob declared.

"About tickling people with sandpaper!" Patrick added.

Chapter 2

There's No Business Like Show Business

SpongeBob quickly ran to the local fast-food restaurant, the Krusty Krab. He wanted to tell his boss, Mr. Krabs, about his idea to make a movie.

"What kind of movie?" asked Mr. Krabs.

"A movie about you, Mr. Krabs!" SpongeBob replied excitedly. "It's called *The Krabfather*."

Mr. Krabs shook his head. "I'm a simple patty man, SpongeBob, not a movie star," he explained.

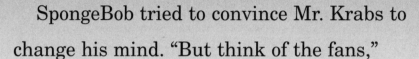

SpongeBob tried to convince Mr. Krabs to change his mind. "But think of the fans," SpongeBob began. "Think of the fame."

Mr. Krabs started to lean forward in his chair.

SpongeBob continued, "Think of . . . the *fortune!*"

Suddenly, Mr. Krabs jumped onto his desk. "Now you're talking my language, SpongeBob!" Mr. Krabs said, shaking SpongeBob's hand. "When do we start?"

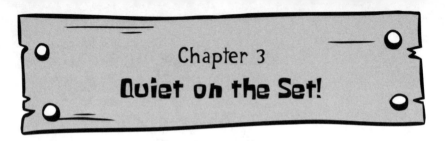

SpongeBob gathered the rest of his cast and crew together. Then he decided it was time to rehearse the first scene.

But Mr. Krabs was growing impatient.

"Let's get started, SpongeBob," Mr. Krabs said. "Money's—I mean—time's a-wasting!"

Suddenly strange music filled the kitchen.

"Cut!" SpongeBob called. "What are you doing, Squidward?"

"There's nothing like good music to add some class to a movie," replied Squidward Tentacles, SpongeBob's neighbor.

"And that, Mr. Squidward, was nothing like good music," Mr. Krabs teased.

Everyone laughed as Squidward stormed off with his clarinet.

Chapter 4
I'm Ready For My Close-up, Mr. SquarePants

SpongeBob asked Mr. Krabs to practice his lines one more time.

"Oh, the joyous life of a fry cook!" sang Mr. Krabs.

"That was great, Mr. Krabs!" SpongeBob told him. "Now we're ready to roll the camera. Action!"

When the camera started rolling, Mr. Krabs started sweating. "Oh, the l-l-life of a fry c-c-c-cook . . . ," he said nervously.

"You can do it, Mr. Krabs," SpongeBob whispered encouragingly.

"Remember, you're the Krabfather!"
SpongeBob added.

But Mr. Krabs became more and more
nervous with every passing second.

"Cut!" SpongeBob finally shouted.

Once the camera stopped, Mr. Krabs instantly felt better. "I'd say that went pretty well, eh, SpongeBob?" he asked.

SpongeBob went home to think about what to do. "Where can I find someone who won't be bothered by the bright lights of fame?" SpongeBob wondered.

"Meow," said his pet snail, Gary.

"I need someone who can carry this movie on his back," SpongeBob said thoughtfully.

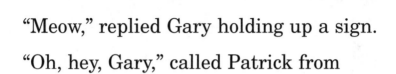

"Meow," replied Gary holding up a sign.

"Oh, hey, Gary," called Patrick from
his house.

"Someone with that genuine *star* quality,"
SpongeBob said to himself,
scratching his head.

"Meow," replied a frustrated Gary.

"Oh, hey, Gary," said Patrick, catching some rays in his beach chair.

"I know!" SpongeBob finally declared. "I'll get Patrick! You know, Gary, I don't know how I do it sometimes."

Chapter 6
Lights! Camera! Action!

So Patrick took Mr. Krabs's place as the star of the movie.

Soon it was time to rehearse again.

"Action!" SpongeBob called.

"Oh, the wife of a fry cook!" Patrick said.

"Patrick, you said *wife* instead of *life,*" SpongeBob explained. "Take two."

"Oh, the knife of the fry cook!" Patrick said.

"Take three."

"Of, fry the cook wife!"

"Take two hundred forty-six!" croaked SpongeBob.

"Frook oh the why life!" said Patrick.

"OH, I CAN'T TAKE IT ANYMORE!"
Patrick finally screamed. He burst through
the wall and ran away.

"Cut!" SpongeBob called. "Now *that's* what
I call acting!"

Chapter 7
Riot on the Set

Soon everyone in Bikini Bottom wanted a
part in SpongeBob's film. So
SpongeBob found a way to include
them all.

When it was time to rehearse his new cast, SpongeBob told them, "Remember, everyone, just ignore the camera. Whatever you do, just act naturally."

But everyone started acting very
un-naturally.

Then Mr. Krabs's arch rival, Plankton,
stepped through the crowd. He started
demanding a larger part.

All of a sudden the crowd turned ugly.
Angry cries of "Me, too," "I'm calling my
agent!" and "What's my motivation?" filled
the water.

Mr. Krabs heard the angry shouts from inside the Krusty Krab. "My money—I mean—my movie's in danger," he cried. "I've got to do something."

Suddenly the restaurant owner got an idea and ran outside.

"I've got one word for you scallywags,"

Mr. Krabs told the crowd. "Lunch!"

Everyone rushed into the Krusty Krab.

"Now start filming, laddie," Mr. Krabs told SpongeBob. "But do it before they realize they're eating the fake Krabby Patties we're using for the movie."

MISTER KRABS PRESENTS

The Krab

Finally, the movie was complete.
"Quiet, everyone!" SpongeBob called from
the audience on opening night. "It's starting!"
"Where's my popcorn?" asked Patrick.

father

a film by SpongeBob SquarePants

Suddenly, strange music filled the theater.

"Down in front, Mr. Squidward!"
Mr. Krabs yelled from the audience.

"You call that acting, Krabs?" Plankton shouted from his seat during Mr. Krabs's scene. "I've seen Krabby Patties with more sizzle than that."

A wave of laughter rippled through the audience.

"This is my best scene," Patrick said proudly, watching himself burst through the wall on screen.

"It's your only scene, Patrick," SpongeBob gently reminded him.

Sandy Cheeks was surprised to see that her friend SpongeBob also played a role in the movie.

"I had no choice," SpongeBob told her.

"The claws wouldn't fit Gary."

"Meow," added Gary.

"Oooh, I look so thin," Mrs. Puff said happily from the audience during the big action scene.

"Oh, why did he have to go so young?"
Mr. Krabs sobbed during the final scene of
the movie.

When the movie ended, the audience
burst into applause.

As they left the theater, Sandy said,
"That was great, SpongeBob!"

"I laughed," Mrs. Puff said.

"I cried," Patrick said.

"Gee, Patrick, I'm touched," SpongeBob replied. "Do you really think the movie was that good?"

"No," Patrick answered. "I dropped my popcorn again!"